A Note from Michelle about
TAP DANCE TROUBLE

Hi! I'm Michelle Tanner. I'm nine years old. And something really great happened to me. I got picked to be in a tap dancing show at the mall. The part that's not so great is that my family can't come to the recital. You see, I twisted my ankle and I kind of told my dad it hurt more than it really did. I got to stay home from school. But now I have to keep my tap dancing a secret from everybody. And that's not going to be easy. Because I live in a very full house!

There's my dad and my two older sisters, D.J. and Stephanie. But that's not all.

My mom died when I was little. So my uncle Jesse moved in to help Dad take care of us. So did Joey Gladstone. He's my dad's friend from college. It's almost like having three dads. But that's still not all!

First Uncle Jesse got married to Becky Donaldson. Then they had twin boys, Nicky and Alex. The twins are four years old now. And they're so cute.

That's nine people. Our dog, Comet, makes ten. Sure, it gets kind of crazy sometimes. But I wouldn't change it for anything. It's so much fun living in a full house!

FULL HOUSE™ MICHELLE novels

The Great Pet Project
The Super-Duper Sleepover Party
My Two Best Friends
Lucky, Lucky Day
The Ghost in My Closet
Ballet Surprise
Major League Trouble
My Fourth-Grade Mess
Bunk 3, Teddy and Me
My Best Friend Is a Movie Star! (Super Special)
The Big Turkey Escape
The Substitute Teacher
Calling All Planets
I've Got a Secret
How to Be Cool
The Not-So-Great Outdoors
My Ho-Ho-Horrible Christmas
My Almost Perfect Plan
April Fools!
My Life Is a Three-Ring Circus
Welcome to My Zoo
The Problem with Pen Pals
Tap Dance Trouble

Activity Book
My Awesome Holiday Friendship Book

Available from MINSTREL Books

FULL HOUSE™
Michelle

Tap Dance Trouble

Cathy East Dubowski

A Parachute Book

A
MINSTREL®
BOOK

Published by POCKET BOOKS
New York   London   Toronto   Sydney   Tokyo   Singapore

A MINSTREL PAPERBACK *Original*

A Minstrel Book published by
POCKET BOOKS, a division of Simon & Schuster Inc.
1230 Avenue of the Americas, New York, NY 10020

A PARACHUTE BOOK

Copyright © and ™ 1999 by Warner Bros.

FULL HOUSE, characters, names and all related indicia are
trademarks of Warner Bros. © 1999.

ISBN: 0-671-02154-0

First Minstrel Books printing January 1999

10 9 8 7 6 5 4 3 2 1

A MINSTREL BOOK and colophon are registered trademarks of
Simon & Schuster Inc.

Cover photo by Schultz Photography

Printed in the U.S.A.

Tap Dance Trouble

Chapter

1

♥ "This is so awesome!" Nine-year-old Michelle Tanner put the final touches on her poster. It was Tuesday morning. Today her fourth-grade class would be showing their projects on the ancient Egyptians.

Michelle glanced at the clock on her dresser. It was seven-thirty. "Uh-oh. Better get ready for school!"

She grabbed her pink and blue backpack and plopped it onto her desk. Then she looked back at the big poster on the floor. I'll have to carry it separately, Michelle decided.

She leaned over her bag and stuffed her books inside. Then she quickly closed it.

Zzziiip!

"Ouch!" Michelle cried. The end of her strawberry-blond hair was caught in her backpack!

She tried jiggling the zipper.

She tried yanking her hair loose. "Ow!"

Stephanie can help, Michelle thought. Her thirteen-year-old sister was blow-drying her hair in the bathroom.

Michelle was halfway out the door when Stephanie rushed into their room.

"Stephanie!" Michelle exclaimed. "Can you help me? My—"

"My hair!" Stephanie shrieked.

"Huh?" Michelle frowned. "What's wrong with *your* hair?"

"Just look at it!" Stephanie moaned. She stared into the mirror above her dresser. "It's all frizzy! It's awful!"

"That's nothing," Michelle replied. "Look at *my* hair! It's stuck! Could you—"

"I'm the one who's *stuck!*" Stephanie wailed, still gazing in the mirror. "Stuck with the worst hair in the universe!" She yanked open her top drawer and dug through her collection of clips, ribbons, and scrunchies.

Michelle sighed and shifted the backpack in her arms. Maybe D.J. can help. Michelle stepped into the hall and yelled for her other sister.

D.J. breezed past Michelle with an armload of books. "Washington, Adams, Jefferson, Madison . . ." D.J. was eighteen and in college. She was always studying.

Too busy studying to notice me, Michelle thought.

She glanced toward the stairs. Uncle Jesse and Aunt Becky lived on the third floor with their four-year-old twins, Alex and Nicky.

"Uncle Jesse," Michelle called as she climbed the steps. "Aunt Becky!"

"Sorry, Michelle," Uncle Jesse said, opening the door a crack. "The twins have colds. You'd better not come up." He closed the door.

Michelle carried her backpack downstairs. Her father was in the kitchen. He was cooking breakfast and talking on the telephone at the same time.

"Dad, my hair—"

"Looks nice, sweetheart," Danny said. He patted her on the head without looking. "What were you saying, Mr. Stevens?" he asked into the phone.

Mr. Stevens worked at the TV station with Michelle's father.

4

I'd better not interrupt, Michelle thought. She rested her backpack on the table and sat down to wait.

Danny had already set out some juice and eggs.

But Michelle smelled something weird. She spotted smoke rising from the shiny toaster on the counter. "Dad! Something's burning!"

Danny quickly unplugged the toaster. Then he plucked out two icky black squares of toast. All while he talked on the phone.

"Argghhh!" Joey Gladstone leaped into the kitchen. He was dressed as a pirate, with a ruffly white shirt and a purple coat with gold buttons. A black patch covered one eye and a gold hoop dangled from his right ear.

Michelle laughed. Joey was her dad's friend. He moved into the basement apartment to help out the family after Michelle's mom died. Joey was a stand-up comedian, and he was always doing something funny.

"Hand over me breakfast!" he cried in a fake pirate voice. He waved a plastic sword in the air. "Or I'll make ye walk the plank!"

"What are you doing in a pirate costume?" Michelle asked, giggling.

"Aye, lassie. I'm working on me pirate jokes," Joey explained. He grabbed a glass of juice. "For a fund-raiser at the children's hospital tonight. Got to practice, matey! See you!"

"But, Joey, wait—"

Slam!

Too late. Joey disappeared down the stairs.

Michelle sighed. "How about you, Comet?" she asked the family's golden retriever, who was gobbling the food in his bowl. "Can you help me with my zipper?"

Comet kept eating. He didn't even look at Michelle.

"That's it!" Michelle shouted.

"I have an announcement! I'm quitting school. I'm running away! I'll never see any of you ever again!"

"That's nice, honey," her father said. He ducked around the phone cord and reached into the refrigerator. "Now, Mr. Stevens, let me explain. . . ."

Michelle slumped down into her chair. *I'm going to have a backpack stuck to my head forever. Well, at least I'll always be ready for school!*

"Hi!" Darcy Powell knocked on the back door and stepped inside the kitchen. She was Stephanie's best friend.

Darcy studied the food on the table. "No banana nut muffins this morning?"

She picked up a fork and scooped some eggs into her mouth. "Hey, Michelle. Did you know your hair is stuck in your backpack," she asked, swallowing.

"No kidding!" Michelle exclaimed. "Can you help me?"

"Sure," Darcy told her. She jiggled the zipper. In seconds Michelle's hair slid free. "There you go."

"Thanks!" Michelle said.

"No problem." Darcy poured some juice into a glass. She drank it down in one long gulp. "Thanks for breakfast. Is Stephanie upstairs?"

Michelle nodded. And Darcy left the kitchen.

Michelle scooped some eggs onto her plate. She gazed out the kitchen window and took a bite. Raindrops pattered onto the glass. "Dad—it's raining."

Danny hung up the phone. "Raining?" he repeated.

"Yes, and I have to take a poster to school," Michelle said. "Can you give me a ride?"

"Sure, honey," Danny replied. He dashed through the house, closing windows.

Michelle heard the school bus roar past. "Dad, we'd better hurry," she said.

"Just let me put the dishes in the dishwasher," Danny replied.

"I'll get my poster." Michelle slipped on her backpack. She picked up her pink and blue lunch box from the counter and went upstairs to her room.

Michelle grabbed the poster off the floor. Then she raced back down to the living room.

"I'm ready, Dad!" she called out.

But everything was quiet.

Where is he? Michelle wondered. "Dad?"

No answer.

Michelle ran to look out the window, and gasped.

Her father had just pulled the family van away from the house.

"Oh, no!" Michelle cried. "Dad left without me!"

Chapter 2

♥ Michelle flopped down on the couch. She let her backpack *thunk* to the floor. She couldn't believe it. Her father totally forgot about her!

Now I'll have to walk to school—in the pouring rain! she thought with a groan. My poster will be ruined. I'll be late. And nobody even cares!

The front door swung open. Danny smiled at her from the doorway. "I knew I forgot *something.*"

Michelle tried not to pout. Dad has a lot of important things on his mind, she told herself. He didn't forget me on purpose.

"I'm sorry, pumpkin." Danny took Michelle's backpack. Together they ducked under his big umbrella and ran to the van.

"So, are you ready for the big jamboree tomorrow?" Danny asked brightly as they drove through the rain to school.

Michelle couldn't help grinning. She had been talking about the Rap-a-Tap-Tap Jamboree all week.

A new dancing school called On Your Toes Dance Studio was opening in the mall. They were holding a big event where kids could sign up to take a free tap lesson. The dancers who showed the most potential would get to be in a show next week.

Michelle was so excited. Her best friends,

Cassie Wilkins and Mandy Metz, were going to try out, too.

"It's going to be so cool! Do you think you can come see me if I'm picked for the show next Saturday?"

"I wouldn't miss it!" Danny assured her.

Danny parked the van in front of the school. Michelle gathered her things.

"Hey, Dad." Michelle held up her lunch box. "This feels really light today. What did you make me for lunch?"

Danny put a hand over his mouth. "Oops. I forgot to make it," he admitted. "I was on the phone and . . ." He fished some dollar bills out of his pocket. "Here." He handed them to her. "You can buy lunch today. Won't that be fun?"

Michelle stared blankly at the crumpled money. She never bought the lunches in the cafeteria. They were gross.

"I guess," Michelle said, and climbed

out of the van. Maybe Mandy will split her sandwich with me, she thought.

The late bell rang.

"Got to go, Dad!" Michelle gave her father a kiss and jumped out of the car.

"Have a good day, pumpkin," Danny called out.

Michelle turned. "I'll try," she cried— just as her foot came down into a huge puddle.

Water splashed all over her socks, her jeans, and her poster.

On second thought, Michelle said to herself, I think it might be too late.

At lunchtime, Michelle poked at the gravy-coated blob of meat loaf on her tray and heaved a big sigh.

Mandy opened her lunch box and took out a tuna sandwich. "What's wrong, Michelle? Is it your poster? Mrs. Yoshida seemed pretty understanding."

"Yeah," Cassie added. "It's not your fault it was raining. We'll help you fix it up."

Michelle shook her head. "Thanks, but that's not it."

"Then, what is it?" Mandy asked.

Michelle explained to them about her stuck zipper. And how everybody in her house had been too busy to help. How they all completely ignored her.

"Then my dad drove off without me," Michelle said, "and forgot to make my lunch!"

"I know how you feel," Mandy told her. She shook her long, curly dark hair. "My family is so big, sometimes my mom can't even keep our names straight!"

"You guys don't know how lucky you

are," Cassie said. "It might be nice *not* to be noticed once in a while."

"You're kidding," Michelle said. "Like when?"

"Like when I break something and there's nobody else to blame!" Cassie said with a giggle.

Michelle laughed. She took a sip from her milk carton.

"Come on, you guys," Mandy announced. "We have more important things to talk about. The Rap-a-Tap-Tap Jamboree starts tomorrow, and we still have to plan what we're going to wear and how we're going to get there."

"I have the perfect outfit picked out," Cassie cried.

"I'll ask my dad to drive us." Michelle smiled. She pushed her tray away. "I think he owes me a favor!"

After everything that happened this

morning, Michelle thought, I'm sure he'll say yes.

That evening Michelle's dad came home late from work. She rushed over to him the minute he came in the door.

"Hey, Dad," Michelle said. "Can I ask you something?"

"Sure, Michelle," he replied. "Just give me a chance to put my things away, okay?" He climbed the stairs to his room.

Aunt Becky walked in the front door a minute later.

"Aunt Becky," Michelle said. She wanted to tell her about the tap show. "Guess what?"

"Hi, Michelle," Aunt Becky replied. "I'll talk to you in a minute, okay?" She raced upstairs.

D.J. and Stephanie were sitting on the couch in front of the television.

"What are you guys watching?" Michelle asked them.

Her sisters didn't answer. They stared at the TV.

Michelle stepped in front of it and waved her arms. *"Hello!"*

"Michelle—move!" Stephanie cried. "They're about to give the answer to the Final Jeopardy question!"

Michelle lowered her head and stepped aside.

Danny came back downstairs, and Michelle followed him into the kitchen. "I have to ask you a question, Dad," she said.

"In a minute, sweetheart," Danny replied, opening cabinets and pulling out pots. "We'll never eat if I don't get dinner started."

Michelle threw up her hands. Why do I even try talking to anyone around here? she wondered. Aunt Becky and Uncle

Jesse are busy with the twins. D.J. and Stephanie are busy with a TV show. Joey's busy doing his pirate jokes. And Dad is busy with everything.

No one has time for me.

Angry tears filled her eyes. Michelle stomped to the stairs. If I stomp loud enough, maybe they'll know how mad I am, she thought.

She wiped the tears away with the back of her hand.

Stomp, stomp, stomp!

I'm going to stomp all the way to my room, Michelle thought, pounding up the steps.

But then she slipped.

She missed the top step.

And Michelle tumbled all the way down the stairs.

"Helllllp!"

Chapter 3

♥ "Michelle!" Stephanie cried.

"What happened?" Danny shouted.

"Are you all right?" D.J. asked.

Michelle lay on the floor at the bottom of the stairs. She was afraid to move. She held her breath as everyone gathered around her.

Then she tried to stand up. Pain shot through her ankle. "Ouch!" she cried.

"Don't move!" Her father knelt beside her. "Tell me where it hurts, sweetheart."

Michelle gulped. She pointed to her ankle. "R-right here."

"I'll get an ice pack," Aunt Becky said.

Danny reached out to touch Michelle's ankle.

"Don't!" she gasped, afraid it would hurt.

"Is it broken, Dad?" Stephanie asked, worried.

"I don't know," her father replied. "Can you wiggle your toes, Michelle?"

Michelle's bottom lip trembled. "I—I don't know." She tried to move her toes just a little. That didn't hurt—too much.

Danny picked Michelle up and carried her to the couch. He propped her foot on a pillow. Then he brushed back her bangs and gave her a gentle kiss on the forehead.

"Stay here," Danny said. "I'm going to call Dr. Stone."

Aunt Becky came back with an ice pack.

"This should make your ankle feel a little better." She placed it on Michelle's ankle.

Michelle jumped. The pack was really cold!

"Here," D.J. said. "Wrap the ice in this towel."

Michelle sighed as Aunt Becky wrapped the ice pack in the soft cloth.

"How does that feel?" Becky asked as she placed the ice on Michelle's leg.

"Better. Thanks, Aunt Becky. Thanks, D.J." Michelle leaned back against the pillow and closed her eyes.

"Oh, Michelle," Stephanie said. "I'm so sorry I yelled at you before."

Huh? Michelle opened one eye. Was Stephanie *apologizing?*

"Can I get you anything?" Stephanie asked her. "Something to make you feel better?"

Stephanie wants to *do* something for

me? Michelle couldn't believe it. That almost *never* happened.

Michelle sighed loudly and nodded. "Maybe . . . a cookie?" she asked her sister.

"You got it!" Stephanie dashed into the kitchen. She returned with a whole plateful of their father's homemade chocolate-chip cookies.

Michelle stuffed one in her mouth—just as Danny came back into the room.

"Uh-oh," she mumbled. Her father had a strict rule: No sweets right before dinner. "Um, I—"

"Don't blame Michelle," Stephanie spoke up quickly. "I gave them to her."

Danny smiled. "It's okay—just this once."

Excellent! Michelle thought. She glanced around at her family. They all looked so worried about her.

"Are you comfortable?" D.J. asked, fluffing the pillow under Michelle's foot.

"I'll get you some milk for your cookies." Stephanie ran back to the kitchen.

Michelle picked up another cookie and took a bite. *Maybe I should hurt my ankle every day!*

"How bad is it, Doctor?" Danny asked anxiously.

Michelle sat on the examining table in Dr. Stone's office.

The doctor moved Michelle's foot in a circle. "Does that hurt?"

Michelle shook her head no.

"How about here?" Dr. Stone asked, touching Michelle's toes.

Michelle shook her head no again.

"Looks like today's your lucky day," Dr. Stone replied. "Your ankle's not broken."

Whew! Michelle was glad about that!

"But you did give it a good twist," the doctor continued. "Putting ice on it right away was a smart thing to do."

Dr. Stone opened a drawer and took out an elastic bandage. "Keep this on as much as possible." She wrapped the bandage snugly around Michelle's ankle. "And stay off your feet for a while."

The doctor turned to Danny. "Give me a call if she has any problems, okay?"

"I will," Danny said.

"One more thing." Dr. Stone slipped a hand into her pocket. "You're not too old for stickers, are you, Michelle?" She pulled out a whole handful to choose from.

Michelle grinned and picked out a shiny unicorn. "Thanks!"

Then Danny carried Michelle to the car. He put her in the front seat.

"I've decided. No school for you tomorrow, young lady," he told her.

All right! Michelle thought. A holiday—just for me!

"Wait here. I'll be right back." Danny shut the car door and dashed inside a nearby store.

A moment later Michelle's father stepped outside with a great big stuffed tiger in his arms. "Here you go," he told her. "I thought this might help you feel better."

Michelle hugged it tight. "Thanks, Dad. I love it!"

Back home, Danny carried Michelle to the couch in the living room. He served her dinner on a tray. Aunt Becky propped her foot up on lots of pillows.

Stephanie turned on the TV and gave Michelle the remote control. "Here, Michelle. You can pick the show we watch."

Wow! Everyone is being so nice to me, Michelle thought. I could get used to this!

Later, Joey performed his whole pirate

routine. And Uncle Jesse played his guitar, and made up a song just for Michelle.

Then D.J. polished Michelle's fingernails with her newest, coolest color.

"Are you all right, Michelle?" they all kept asking.

"Can I get you anything, Michelle?"

"Do you want anything else to drink, Michelle?"

Michelle sank back into her pillows and hugged her cuddly new tiger. She hadn't had so much fun in a long time. She felt like a queen.

"This is the life!" She sighed.

Chapter 4

♥ The next morning Michelle woke up in her bed.

Hey! she thought, looking around. How did I get up here?

The last thing she remembered was watching an old movie on TV with her dad.

I must have fallen asleep on the couch. Dad probably carried me up to bed. She grinned at her new stuffed tiger tucked in bed beside her.

Michelle stretched, and wiggled her toes. Carefully she moved her foot in a circle—just as Dr. Stone had done. Her ankle felt a lot better.

"I bet I can walk." She threw back the covers and sat up.

"Good morning!" Danny called. He came in the room, carrying a breakfast tray. "How are you feeling?"

"I'm—"

Michelle stopped herself. She was about to tell her dad that she was fine. But then she remembered what a great time she'd had the night before. How nice everyone had been to her. And today she was supposed to stay home from school. . . .

Maybe I should pretend—just a little, she told herself.

"Well . . ." Michelle said slowly. "Let's see if I can walk."

She swung her legs out of bed and limped slowly around the room. "Owwww!"

"Hold it right there!" Danny shook his head and set the tray on her desk. "Let me help you back into bed. We don't want to take any chances with your ankle."

Michelle snuggled under the covers. "You're the boss," she said.

"You're right," Danny replied. "And I've already called the school and told them you'll be absent today. So it's all settled." He placed the breakfast tray in front of her.

"Mmm," Michelle said. "French toast, my favorite!"

There was milk and fresh-squeezed orange juice, too. A glass vase with a pink rose. Even a cloth napkin like the ones they used on holidays.

This is so cool, Michelle thought.

"I have to go to work now," Danny told

her. "But Uncle Jesse will be here all morning. I'll be home around lunchtime to check up on you, okay?"

He stepped into the hall for a moment. He came back with two crutches in his hands. "I bought these this morning," Danny explained. "Use them if you have to get up. But I really want you to stay off that foot. Understand?"

"Sure, Dad," Michelle said through a mouthful of food.

Danny pulled out a small brass bell from his pocket. "Ring this if you need anything."

Excellent! Michelle thought. She gave the bell a test shake.

Ring-a-ling!

Michelle could hear Uncle Jesse pounding down the stairs from the third floor.

"You rang?" he asked as he hurried into the room.

Michelle gave her dad the thumbs-up sign.

"Need anything, kiddo?" Uncle Jesse asked.

Michelle looked over her tray. "More syrup, please," she said with a grin.

Uncle Jesse folded his hands together and bowed like a genie. "Your wish is my command," he said.

After Michelle finished breakfast she rang the little bell again. Uncle Jessie carried her downstairs to the living room so she could watch TV.

"Are you sure you don't mind, Uncle Jesse?" she asked later when she rang for another pillow. "I know you have to take care of the twins upstairs."

"Mind?" Uncle Jesse said, gasping. He shook his head. "You're saving me money!"

"Really?" Michelle asked. "How?"

Uncle Jesse pointed to the stairs. "Some

people pay a gym lots of money for the workout I'm getting today."

Michelle giggled.

"Daddy!" Nicky called.

"We need you!" Alex cried.

Uncle Jesse took a deep breath. "I bet I could even try out for the Olympics after this!"

Danny came home at lunchtime with a pizza, ice cream, and a new book.

When Danny went back to work, Michelle curled up on the couch and read.

Then Michelle closed her eyes.

The next thing she knew, someone was tapping her on the shoulder.

"Michelle," she heard Cassie whisper.

"Are you asleep?" Mandy asked softly.

Michelle kept her eyes shut. "Yes," she whispered sleepily.

Cassie laughed and hit Michelle playfully with a pillow. "We brought you your homework."

"Thanks a *lot!*" Michelle's eyes popped open.

"Hey, what's this bell for?" Cassie held it up and shook it.

Ring-a-ling-ling!

"That's how I call Uncle Jesse if I need anything," Michelle explained.

Cassie giggled. "Cool."

"So how are you feeling?" Mandy asked.

Michelle moved her foot in a circle again. Her ankle was feeling much better. Almost perfect. "Well, to tell you the truth—"

"You need something, Michelle?" Uncle Jesse raced down the stairs. "I heard the bell."

"Oops! Sorry," Cassie said. "I accidentally rang it."

"No problem." Uncle Jesse panted as he

plopped down into a big armchair. "But I think I need a rest."

"What were you going to say, Michelle?" Cassie asked, turning to her.

Michelle gulped. She was about to tell her friends the truth. That her ankle didn't really hurt. That she was pretending. Just so she could stay home from school—and get lots of attention. But how could she tell them now—with Uncle Jesse listening?

"Um . . . nothing," she replied at last.

"It's too bad you hurt your ankle," Mandy said.

"Yeah," Cassie agreed. "You must be so disappointed."

"Disappointed?" Michelle asked. "How come?"

"Yeah, how come?" Uncle Jesse repeated.

"Because of the Rap-a-Tap-Tap Jamboree," Cassie replied. "It starts today, remember? That's another reason we came by. To see if you could come with us. But now that you twisted your ankle, you'll have to miss the whole thing."

Oh, no! Michelle's heart sank. The jamboree!

How could I forget about that?

Chapter

5

♥ "I—I—" Michelle didn't know what to say.

She glanced at Uncle Jesse. He had run up and down the stairs all day for her. And he hadn't complained once.

Michelle really wanted to go to the tap tryouts. But she couldn't tell her friends she'd been faking. Not in front of Uncle Jesse!

What was she going to do?

"I'm really feeling a lot better," she began, smiling at Uncle Jesse. "Maybe I could still go?"

Jesse leaped to his feet. "No way!"

"But, Uncle Jesse—"

"You can't dance on that ankle," Jesse said. "I'm sorry, Michelle.

What am I going to do? Michelle thought again. I can't miss the jamboree. I just can't!

She had to think of something—quick!

"Maybe I could just go and watch," she suggested.

"That's a great idea," Cassie said.

"We promise to take good care of her," Mandy added. "And my mom's driving. She's right outside."

Uncle Jesse shook his head. "I don't know . . ."

"Come on, Uncle Jesse," Michelle

begged. "I'm really much better. And I'll just watch. Pleeaase!"

"Yeah, pleeaase!" Cassie chimed in.

"Well . . . okay," Uncle Jesse said slowly. "But whatever you do, stay off that ankle!"

Tap-tap-tap. Shuffle-tap-tap! STOMP!
The dance teachers from the On Your Toes Dance Studio had set up a stage in the middle of the mall. Some of them were dancing to draw a crowd. A bunch of kids were waiting to sign up.

Mandy and Cassie helped Michelle sit on a folding chair near the stage.

"You'll be able to see everything from here," Mandy said.

Michelle watched her friends run over to a tall, slim woman holding a clipboard. She wore a black body suit and pale pink tights. Her hair was wrapped into a tight bun.

"Hello, students," the woman said into a microphone. "My name is Diana Claybourne. Welcome to the Rap-a-Tap-Tap Jamboree! Are you all ready to dance?"

The kids cheered and clapped.

Michelle clapped, too. She wanted to jump right onto the stage, but she knew she couldn't.

Diana handed each kid a pair of tap shoes. Then she divided the students into groups of five.

Soon the music began. Each group started tapping.

Michelle bobbed her head to the music. She moved her foot to the rhythm as she watched the kids dance.

She remembered a lot of the steps from when she took tap lessons. And Cassie and Mandy were doing great!

Tap-tap-tap. Shuffle-tap-tap STOMP!

Michelle wished more than anything that she could be up on that stage with them.

"Hey, Michelle!" Cassie cried from the stage. "Look at me!"

Tap-tap-tap. Shuffle-tap-tap STOMP!

"Way to go, Cassie!" Michelle yelled. She leaped out of her seat.

She did a quick tap-shuffle-stomp step and clapped for her friend.

Cassie and Mandy stared at Michelle in shock.

"Oops. Busted," Michelle whispered.

Chapter
6

♥ Cassie and Mandy rushed over to Michelle. Their tap shoes clicked on the tile floor.

"Michelle!" Mandy gasped.

"Are you okay?" Cassie asked.

Michelle felt her face turn red. She couldn't lie to her friends. She took a deep breath and blurted out the whole story.

"Everyone was being so nice to me," she told them. "I got presents. I stayed home from school. I had breakfast in bed, and ate pizza for lunch. That's why I let everyone think my ankle hurt worse than it really did."

Cassie and Mandy didn't say a word.

Michelle glanced at her crutches. "Are you guys mad at me?"

"Are you *kidding?*" Mandy cried. "This is great!"

"Now you can dance!" Cassie added. "Come on!"

Michelle followed Cassie and Mandy to the stage. Diana added Michelle's name to the list. She gave Michelle a name tag and let her pick out a pair of tap shoes.

"Okay, kids," Diana called out. "Let's take it from the top. And put some heart into it!"

Michelle watched Diana closely and copied all the steps.

Shuffle with the right foot, shuffle with the left. "I'm doing it!" Michelle shouted.

A big grin spread across her face. She loved the sound her shoes made as they tapped in time to the music. "This is fun!"

Halfway through the practice, Diana turned the class over to another teacher and watched the students as they danced.

Diana must be picking the kids who will be in the show next week, Michelle thought. She flashed Diana a big smile.

When the music stopped, Diana called a break.

Michelle grinned at Cassie and Mandy. What could be more fun than tap dancing with your two best friends?

Then something out in the mall caught her eye. A girl with long, blond hair was gazing into a store called Bizarre Bazaar.

Michelle gasped and ducked behind Cassie.

"Michelle, what are you doing?" Cassie asked.

"It's Stephanie!" Michelle whispered back. "She can't see me! She'll tell my dad about my ankle before I have time to explain."

"She's turning this way!" Mandy cried. "What do we do?"

Michelle held her breath as the girl spun around. Then Michelle saw her face. It wasn't Stephanie.

"That was close!" Cassie said. "But you'll have to tell your family anyway. Now that you're in the jamboree."

"I know," Michelle agreed.

"Okay, everyone," Diana called out over the microphone. "Sit down, please. We're going to give out parts for the show on Saturday."

"Good luck!" Michelle whispered to her friends.

She crossed her fingers.

"The chorus," Diana explained, "is a group of dancers who all do the same thing at the same time."

One by one Diana called out the names of the kids who would be in the chorus.

Michelle waited excitedly for her name to be called.

But Diana didn't call Michelle. Or Mandy. Or even Cassie.

Michelle's heart sank.

"Does this mean we're not going to be in the show?" Cassie whispered.

"I don't know," Mandy answered.

"Now for the special parts," Diana announced.

"*Special* parts?" Michelle's eyes opened wide. She grabbed her friends' hands. "Maybe that's us!"

Cassie covered her ears. "I can't listen. I'm too nervous!"

"The following dancers will do a special number in the show," Diana said. "Michael Banim, Jennifer Edwin, Mandy Metz . . ."

"Mandy! All right!" Michelle gave her friend a high-five.

Then she crossed her fingers.

"Kenny Price, Michelle Tanner, and Cassie Wilkins."

"Yes!" Michelle pumped her fist in the air. "We all made it!"

Michelle, Cassie, and Mandy spent the rest of the lesson learning their special parts. There were a lot of steps to remember, but Michelle was determined to learn them all.

"It's a lot to know by next Saturday," Diana announced when the class was over. "But you'll all be great if you practice as much as you can at home."

No problem, Michelle said to herself. I'll practice all night long!

Michelle spent the ride home thinking of how she was going to tell her family the good news. And how she was going to tell them her ankle was okay.

Mrs. Metz stopped the car in front of Michelle's house. "I'm so glad you're feeling better," she said as Michelle jumped out.

"So am I!" Michelle replied. "Thanks for the ride!"

Mandy handed Michelle her crutches. "See you tomorrow."

"Good luck with you-know-what," Cassie whispered.

"Thanks!" Michelle flew up the steps to her house.

She tried to push the door open. It didn't budge. "That's weird," Michelle said. "It's locked."

Michelle didn't have a key. She rang the doorbell.

I'll just say it was a twenty-four-hour sprain, she decided as she waited for someone to answer the door.

No, Michelle thought. I can tell them it was those vitamins Dad made me start taking last week!

Michelle waited in front of the door. Why isn't anyone answering the bell? she wondered.

She pressed it again.

Ding-dong. Ding-dong.

The door swung open.

Party horns blared.

Her father and sisters stood grinning in the doorway.

"Surprise!" they shouted.

Chapter

7

♥ Michelle dropped her crutches. They clattered onto the floor.

She stared into the living room with her mouth open.

There stood her whole family, laughing and smiling at her. She gazed at the colorful banner hanging across the room. It read: WE LOVE YOU, MICHELLE!

"Michelle!" her father exclaimed. "Your crutches!" He rushed to her side and scooped her up into his arms. Then he placed her carefully on the couch.

"Dad—" Michelle began.

"You've been such a good sport about this all," Danny interrupted her. "Especially about not being in the jamboree. We thought you deserved something really special. So I made your favorite dinner for you."

"And I rented your all-time-favorite video," Joey added.

The twins jumped onto the couch beside her. They waved some papers in her face. "Look what we colored for you, Michelle!" Nicky cried.

They must be feeling better, too, Michelle thought.

"Careful, you guys," Aunt Becky warned. "We don't want to hurt Michelle's *other* ankle!"

"Thanks, guys," Michelle said. "This is really nice, but I have to tell you—"

"First look at what D.J. and I got for you," Stephanie said. She knelt down in front of the couch and handed Michelle a shiny purple package.

"A present?" Michelle tore off the paper. It was a book on how to make friendship bracelets.

"Thank you!" Michelle cried. She gave her sisters a hug.

But inside she felt terrible. She didn't deserve their present. She didn't deserve any of this. She wasn't even hurt anymore.

"You shouldn't have," Michelle told them. "Really."

"But we know how disappointed you must be," D.J. told her.

"You do?" Michelle asked.

"Of course," Stephanie said. "It must

have been torture watching Cassie and Mandy at the mall."

"Knowing that you couldn't be in the tap show," D.J. added.

"But that's what I'm trying to tell you!" Michelle said.

Her father smiled. "What, pumpkin?"

The truth, Michelle told herself. My ankle's fine. Just say it!

Michelle swallowed. "What I wanted to say was . . ."

"Go on," Aunt Becky said, tucking another pillow behind Michelle's back.

Joey handed her a glass of lemonade. "Yeah, Michelle, go on."

"What kind of cake are we having, Uncle Danny?" Nicky asked.

"Shhh! It's a secret, remember?" Alex whispered to Nicky. "Chocolate! Michelle's favorite."

Michelle put her hand to her forehead. This was getting worse by the minute!

"Go ahead, sweetheart," Danny said. "You were going to tell us something."

"I just wanted to say . . ." Michelle looked at her family. At everyone who had gone out of their way to make her feel special.

How can I tell them I'm a faker? After all this? she wondered.

Michelle shook her head. "I just wanted to say . . . thanks."

"You're welcome, Michelle." Danny gave her a squeeze. "Now, let's eat!"

Joey dragged a chair out from the kitchen. "Your chariot awaits, my lady!" He lifted Michelle onto it. Uncle Jesse got on the other side. And together they carried her into the kitchen.

Michelle couldn't believe her eyes. The table had all her favorite foods on it.

"Are you cheered up yet?" Nicky asked from across the table.

Michelle nodded and tried to smile. But inside she felt awful.

I'm a big phony, she thought. But telling them now will spoil their whole party.

She took a sip of her lemonade. I'll tell them tomorrow, she promised herself.

Tomorrow. For sure.

Chapter

8

♥ "Dad, I'm fine." Michelle said to her father the next morning. "Really."

Danny was sitting on the edge of the bed, checking her ankle. "Don't rush it, Michelle," he told her. "You have to be careful with these things."

"But I'm better," Michelle insisted. "I think I can go to school today. And even go to the jamboree at the mall."

Danny gazed at Michelle. "I know how

much you wanted to be in the jamboree. But I'm afraid you're just going to have to forget about it. Maybe they'll do it again next year."

"But, Dad—" Michelle began.

"You can go back to school," he continued. "But you have to use your crutches. At least for the first day."

Crutches at school? Michelle frowned. "Ugh!"

"Michelle!" her father gasped. "What happened? Where does it hurt?"

"Nowhere," Michelle said.

"Don't try to cover it up, sweetheart," he said. "You don't have to pretend with me."

Michelle groaned. Her dad was not making this easy. "My ankle feels fine," she told him. "I promise."

Danny nodded, but Michelle could tell he didn't believe her.

"Do you think you can get dressed by yourself, and make it downstairs?" he asked. "I baked some blueberry muffins for breakfast. And when you're finished eating, I'll drive you to school. How does that sound?"

"Sounds great, Dad," Michelle replied.

Michelle was ten minutes late when she arrived at Mrs. Yoshida's room. Danny had insisted on walking her to class. The rest of the kids were already in their seats.

"What happened to you?" Lee Wagner asked when he saw her come in.

"She probably tripped over her own feet," Jeff Farrington said.

A couple of kids laughed.

Michelle's cheeks burned as the class watched her hobble across the room on her crutches.

Danny helped Michelle to her seat and set down her backpack and lunch box.

"Don't worry, Mr. Tanner," Mrs. Yo-shida said. "We'll take good care of her."

"I guess you didn't tell your family yet, huh?" Cassie whispered to Michelle.

Michelle shook her head. "But look what Aunt Becky and Uncle Jesse got me!" She stuck out her foot. Her bandage was covered with glitter stickers.

"Awesome!" Mandy said from the next row.

"And look at these crutches," Michelle added. Pink and blue ribbons streamed down from the handles.

"Stephanie and D.J. decorated them after I went to sleep last night," Michelle explained.

"But what about the jamboree?" Cassie asked her. "Will you have to quit now?"

"No way!" Michelle said quickly.

"But how can you keep going?" Mandy asked. "And how can you practice? I practiced for almost an hour last night. And I still don't have the steps right."

"Me, too," Cassie said. "What about you, Michelle? Did you get to practice at all?"

Michelle shook her head. "Not with everyone thinking I was hurt. They even threw me a big party last night. Just because they thought I was missing the jamboree."

"So what are you going to do?" Mandy asked.

Michelle shrugged. "I guess I won't practice," she said. "I'll have to sneak over to the mall and learn the dance there. At least until I think of a way to straighten this out."

"Michelle," Mrs. Yoshida said at lunchtime. "Why don't you come to the front of the line so I can help you. Lee, would you please carry Michelle's lunch box for her?"

Usually Michelle liked to walk next to Mrs. Yoshida.

Not today, though.

All her classmates stared as she swung to the front of the line on her crutches. Can they tell I'm pretending? Michelle wondered nervously. What if someone calls me a faker?

"All right, class," Mrs. Yoshida said. "Let's go." She turned off the light and led the students down to the lunchroom.

Michelle wasn't used to walking on crutches. She walked very slowly.

"Hurry up, Michelle," she heard Jeff call out. "It'll be dinnertime when we get to the lunchroom!"

"I hope we get there before all the food is gone," Anna Abdul whispered loudly.

"Don't listen to them, Michelle," Mandy told her.

Michelle couldn't help it. This wasn't the kind of attention she liked.

After lunch, Mr. Gates, the gym teacher, led Michelle's class onto the playground.

The sun was shining. It was a beautiful day. Michelle felt like running. But she couldn't.

"Move it, Tanner!" Jonathan Bennett shouted as he picked up a large red ball. "You're in the way!" He kicked the ball to Lee.

"Why don't you sit down over here, Michelle." Mr. Gates pointed to a nearby bench. Then he blew his whistle. "All right, the rest of you, let's go!"

"This stinks!" Michelle muttered. "I love kick ball." She propped her crutches against the bench and stretched her bandaged foot in front of her.

Michelle's class formed two teams. Cassie and Mandy were on the same team. They waved to Michelle.

Michelle waved back glumly.

It was fun faking a sprained ankle at home. Her family was worried about her. They did things to make her feel special.

But it's not fun being stuck on crutches at school, Michelle decided.

She didn't like people complaining about her. She didn't like being slow and in the way. And she *didn't* like missing out on gym.

If only—

"Watch out!" Michelle heard Mandy scream.

Michelle looked up.

A kick ball was flying straight toward her!

Chapter 9

❤ *WHACK!*

Michelle smacked the ball with one of her crutches—without even getting up.

The ball sailed back across the field.

"All right, Michelle," Cassie cheered. "Score one for our team!"

"Yes!" Michelle pumped the air with her fist. "Am I good at kick ball, or what!"

"No fair," Jeff complained. "You can't use a stick in kick ball!"

"Michelle's not even on their team," Jonathan shouted.

Mr. Gates blew his whistle. "Settle down, everyone!" He strode over to Michelle. "I think you'd better go inside," he said.

"Why, Mr. Gates?" Michelle asked. "Please, can't I stay?"

"I'm sorry," he said kindly. "But it's a little rough out here on the playground. I don't want you to get hurt."

Michelle grabbed her crutches and slowly made her way across the field. When she reached the school door she turned to see the rest of her class starting the game again.

This is the pits, she thought miserably. I've got to get myself out of this mess— soon!

Michelle, Cassie, and Mandy hurried to the stage in the middle of the mall that Monday.

Michelle pulled her tap shoes out of her backpack and slipped them on.

She felt guilty for sneaking to the mall after school. But Michelle had it all planned. Tonight, at dinner, she would tell her family the truth.

Diana led the dancers through the chorus steps. Then she called the special dancers to the front. She gave each kid a shiny black cane.

"I'm not going to dance with you today," Diana told the group. "I want to see how you're doing on your own."

Diana turned on the music. Michelle tried to think of the steps to the dance. But she couldn't remember how they went!

I wish I could have practiced last night, she thought. What am I going to do?

She watched Cassie and Mandy's feet and tried to copy them.

Tap-tap-tap. Shuffle-tap . . .

CRASH!

Michelle smashed into Cassie. She had turned right when everyone else had gone left.

"Sorry," Michelle mumbled.

Diana stopped the music. "Let's take it from the top again," she said, resetting the record.

Once again Michelle glanced nervously up and down the line. She tried to follow the other dancers.

What were the steps? What was she supposed to do?

Michelle couldn't remember.

"Michelle!" Mandy whispered. "Over here!"

Michelle ran over to Mandy and tried to catch up.

Michelle kicked out her left foot.

"Ow!" Mandy squealed.

Then Michelle tripped over another girl's cane.

"Whoa—whoa!" Michelle tried to catch her balance.

It was too late.

She grabbed the other girl's arm. They both tumbled to the ground.

"Hold it! Hold it!" Diana called out. She rubbed her forehead and switched off the music.

Michelle's heard a few girls snicker.

"Okay," Diana said. "Five-minute break. Everybody get some water."

Michelle's face grew hot. This is so embarrassing, she thought as she headed to the water fountain.

Then she felt a hand on her shoulder.

"Are you okay?" Diana asked her.

Michelle turned around. "I think so," she said. "I'm sorry I messed up."

"Michelle, did you practice last night?" Diana asked.

"Well . . ." Michelle answered. "You see . . ."

Diana stared at her.

"Not much," Michelle admitted.

"Michelle," Diana said. "If you're going to be in the show on Saturday, you'll have to practice at home."

Michelle hung her head. "I know."

"If you can't do the steps," Diana went on, "you can't be in the show."

Michelle's head jerked. Not be in the show? No way!

"I'll practice," Michelle said. "I promise!"

Chapter

10

♥ All the way home Michelle thought about what Diana said. I have to learn those steps, she told herself. I have to practice—now!

Michelle hurried up to her room and shut the door. Thank goodness Stephanie wasn't there.

She slipped on the shiny black tap shoes Diana had given her and danced a few warm-up steps.

Tap-tap-tap-tap-tap-tap!

"Michelle!" her father shouted from downstairs. "What's that noise?"

Oh, no! He can hear me! Michelle didn't want her father to find out about the tap show. Not until she explained about her ankle.

"Uh, nothing, Dad!" Michelle yelled back.

How am I going to practice without making noise? She flopped down on her bed and hugged her pillow.

"That's it," Michelle cried. "Pillows! I'll tie them to my feet. Dad won't hear a thing."

She grabbed the two pillows from her bed and placed them on the floor. Then Michelle took two belts from her closet. She stepped on the pillows. And tied them to her feet with the belts.

Michelle stood in front of a full-length

71

mirror. She hummed the dance music. Then she began to do the steps.

Fwump-fwump-fwump.

Michelle smothered a giggle with her hands. She felt as if she were tap-dancing on giant marshmallows!

Fwump-fwump-fwump.

She pictured where she would be standing on the stage. Imagined the lights on her face. The parents and shoppers who would crowd around to watch.

Fwump-fwump-fwump. Shuffle-fwump . . . THUD!

The bedroom door flew open. "Michelle, what are you doing?" Danny's head poked into the room.

Michelle froze.

Her father glanced at her feet. "What's going on?"

It's time to tell the truth, Michelle decided.

"I'm practicing for the Rap-a-Tap-Tap Jamboree," she told him.

"Oh, Michelle . . ." Her dad came over and gave her a hug. "You are the most determined little girl I have ever known. And I'm proud of you. But you know you can't dance on Saturday."

"But, Dad, I can. I'm better," Michelle insisted. "My ankle doesn't hurt. Really. See?"

Fwump-fwump-fwump.

She did a few steps for him.

"Oh, really?" Danny said gently. "Then why are you tapping with pillows on your feet?"

Michelle couldn't believe it. She knew she shouldn't have faked being hurt. Now she wanted to tell the truth—and her dad wouldn't believe her!

"Dad, listen—"

"No, Michelle," he said finally. He made

73

her sit on her bed. Then he removed the pillows and tap shoes from Michelle's feet. "Take it easy. And stay off that ankle! I'll be in the laundry room doing some ironing if you need me. Just ring your bell."

Before Michelle could say another word, he was gone.

Michelle jumped out of bed. I'll just have to prove that I'm okay!

She slipped on the tap shoes and raced downstairs. When she got to the kitchen, she stopped.

Everyone who's home will have to hear me here, Michelle thought. Once I start tapping, they'll all come in and see that I'm fine.

Happily, Michelle began to dance.

Tap-tap-tap. Shuffle-tap-tap-STOMP!

Nobody came.

Michelle started tapping faster.

Tap-Tap-Tap. Shuffle-tap-STOMP!

"Look at me! I'm dancing!" Michelle shouted. She swung her arms around and around.

BONK!

CRASH!

Michelle knocked a vase off the kitchen counter. It landed right on her foot.

"Ow! Ow! Ow!" Michelle shouted.

Danny rushed into the kitchen. Aunt Becky and Uncle Jesse followed close behind.

"Michelle!" Danny cried. "What happened? Are you hurt?"

Michelle was hopping up and down, holding one foot. "I'm okay," Michelle said. "It's no big deal."

"Yes it is!" Her father scooped her into his arms. "I knew I let you back on your feet too soon."

"But, Dad—"

"No buts," Danny said, carrying Michelle up to her room. Then he shook his head and sighed. "Oh, Michelle, what am I going to do with you?"

The jamboree is on Saturday, Michelle thought. What am *I* going to do?

Chapter
11

♥ "Okay, everyone," Diana called out. "You're looking really good. Take a break."

It was Saturday morning at the mall—the last rehearsal for the Rap-a-Tap-Tap Jamboree.

Diana gave all the dancers black top hats with bright red bands. She passed out black jackets, red bow ties, and shiny black canes.

Michelle had practiced that week at Cassie's house—every day after school. Today Mandy's mom drove them to the mall early so they could practice some more.

Diana walked over to Michelle and her friends. "I'm so proud of you girls!" she said warmly. "Michelle—I can really tell that you've been practicing."

Michelle beamed.

"Do you really think we're good?" Cassie asked her.

"More than that," Diana said. "You girls look like you're having so much fun when you tap."

"We are," Michelle said.

"Well, get ready, girls," she said. "We'll be starting the show soon."

"Oh, look!" Cassie said. "There's my mom and dad!" She jumped off the stage to give them a hug before the show.

Mandy ran over to her family to model her costume for them.

Michelle watched her friends with their families. And suddenly her excitement faded.

I wish my family could be here, too, Michelle thought sadly. It's just not the same without them here to see me.

It's my own fault, she admitted. I shouldn't have pretended my foot was hurt.

Michelle sat on the edge of the stage.

A few moments later, Diana sat beside her. "Michelle, what's wrong?" she asked.

"Oh, nothing," Michelle said. "Just nervous, I guess."

"You'll do great," Diana said. "And I'd love to have you in one of my regular classes. You have a lot of potential."

Michelle sat up. "Really?"

Diana nodded and stood up. "Really. Think about it. Okay?"

"I will!"

Wow! Michelle thought as Diana hopped off the stage. Diana thinks I'm really good. I should be feeling wonderful.

So why do I still feel so bad?

Michelle gazed at Cassie and her parents. At Mandy with the whole Metz family.

She knew why.

Michelle was getting ready to dance— but what good was it without her family there to see her?

How did things get so messed up? Michelle wondered sadly. She wandered over to the water fountain and took a drink.

When she stood up, she bumped into someone behind her.

She turned around to say excuse me.

But the words got stuck in her throat.

Danny Tanner stood there. He folded his arms across his chest. "Michelle, what are you doing here?"

Chapter 12

♥ "Uh, hi, Dad," Michelle stammered. "Funny meeting you here!"

Danny glanced down at her tap shoes. He stared at her costume.

Her father was giving her *the look*. The look that meant he was going to stand there and wait until she explained everything.

No more excuses, Michelle said to herself.

She told him everything. How she felt

as if no one noticed her. How great it was when she hurt her ankle, and everyone made her feel special.

"Everything got all tangled up," Michelle said. "And when I finally tried to tell the truth, nobody believed me."

Danny placed his hand on Michelle's shoulder. "We live in a pretty full house, Michelle. There's a lot going on. I'm sorry we didn't pay attention to you. And I'm sorry we didn't listen."

"I know you're busy, Dad," Michelle said.

"But I should never be too busy for you," Danny admitted. He gave her a hug.

"However," her father went on. "There is still the matter of your sneaking off to the mall."

"Oh, yeah, that," Michelle said.

"Maybe we should go home and talk about it," Danny suggested.

"No, Dad, please! You have every right to be mad at me," Michelle said. "But it's almost time for the show. And Diana says I'm pretty good. I even have a special part!"

"Really? Well then, I guess we can't miss that, can we?" Danny replied. "But that doesn't mean you're off the hook for sneaking out."

"I know," Michelle said. "Thanks for letting me be in the show."

Danny grinned and nodded. "And we'll all watch you." He pointed toward the rows of folding chairs where Stephanie, D.J., Uncle Joey, Aunt Becky, Uncle Jesse, Nicky, and Alex waited for the show to begin.

Michelle couldn't believe it. Her whole

family was going to see her in the show after all!

"But I don't understand," Michelle said. "Why is everyone here at the mall?"

"Well, I got worried when I couldn't find you this morning!" Danny explained. "I called Mrs. Metz, and she told me you were in the show. So I gathered everybody together and brought them here to see you."

"Welcome, friends and family, to the Rap-a-Tap-Tap Jamboree!" a voice boomed across the mall.

Michelle turned back to the stage. Diana was at the microphone. The dancers lined up behind her.

Danny gave Michelle another quick hug. "Break a leg," he told her. "Just don't sprain an ankle!"

Michelle laughed. Then she ran to join the others.

"Is that your family out there?" Mandy whispered when Michelle stepped into place beside her.

Michelle spotted Nicky and Alex waving to her from the audience. "Uh-huh. They're all here."

"Then everything's all right?" Cassie asked.

"Better than all right," Michelle said. "Everything's perfect."

Just last week she thought her family didn't notice her—that they didn't care.

Now I know they really do care, Michelle said to herself. And they always will.

Then the music began.

Michelle put her best foot forward. With her whole family watching, she didn't miss a step.

FULL HOUSE™
SISTERS

A brand-new series starring Stephanie AND Michelle!

#1 Two On The Town

Stephanie and Michelle find themselves
in the big city—and in big trouble!

#2 One Boss Too Many

Stephanie and Michelle think camp will be major fun.
If only these two sisters were getting along!

When sisters get together...expect the unexpected!

A MINSTREL® BOOK
Published by Pocket Books

2012-01

FULL HOUSE Stephanie™

PHONE CALL FROM A FLAMINGO	88004-7/$3.99
THE BOY-OH-BOY NEXT DOOR	88121-3/$3.99
TWIN TROUBLES	88290-2/$3.99
HIP HOP TILL YOU DROP	88291-0/$3.99
HERE COMES THE BRAND NEW ME	89858-2/$3.99
THE SECRET'S OUT	89859-0/$3.99
DADDY'S NOT-SO-LITTLE GIRL	89860-4/$3.99
P.S. FRIENDS FOREVER	89861-2/$3.99
GETTING EVEN WITH THE FLAMINGOES	52273-6/$3.99
THE DUDE OF MY DREAMS	52274-4/$3.99
BACK-TO-SCHOOL COOL	52275-2/$3.99
PICTURE ME FAMOUS	52276-0/$3.99
TWO-FOR-ONE CHRISTMAS FUN	53546-3/$3.99
THE BIG FIX-UP MIX-UP	53547-1/$3.99
TEN WAYS TO WRECK A DATE	53548-X/$3.99
WISH UPON A VCR	53549-8/$3.99
DOUBLES OR NOTHING	56841-8/$3.99
SUGAR AND SPICE ADVICE	56842-6/$3.99
NEVER TRUST A FLAMINGO	56843-4/$3.99
THE TRUTH ABOUT BOYS	00361-5/$3.99
CRAZY ABOUT THE FUTURE	00362-3/$3.99
MY SECRET ADMIRER	00363-1/$3.99
BLUE RIBBON CHRISTMAS	00830-7/$3.99
THE STORY ON OLDER BOYS	00831-5/$3.99
MY THREE WEEKS AS A SPY	00832-3/$3.99
NO BUSINESS LIKE SHOW BUSINESS	01725-X/$3.99
MAIL ORDER BROTHER	01726-8/$3.99
TO CHEAT OR NOT TO CHEAT	01727-6/$3.99
WINNING IS EVERYTHING	02098-6/$3.99

Available from Minstrel® Books Published by Pocket Books

It doesn't matter if you live around the corner...
or around the world...
If you are a fan of Mary-Kate and Ashley Olsen,
you should be a member of

MARY-KATE + ASHLEY'S FUN CLUB™

Here's what you get:
Our Funzine™
An autographed color photo
Two black & white individual photos
A full size color poster
An official **Fun Club**™ membership card
A **Fun Club**™ school folder
Two special **Fun Club**™ surprises
A holiday card
Fun Club™ collectibles catalog
Plus a **Fun Club**™ box to keep everything in

To join Mary-Kate + Ashley's Fun Club™, fill out the form
below and send it along with

U.S. Residents – $17.00
Canadian Residents – $22 U.S. Funds
International Residents – $27 U.S. Funds

**MARY-KATE + ASHLEY'S FUN CLUB™
859 HOLLYWOOD WAY, SUITE 275
BURBANK, CA 91505**

NAME:_____

ADDRESS:_____

_CITY:_____ STATE:_____ ZIP:_____

PHONE:(____) _____ BIRTHDATE:_____

1242

FULL HOUSE™
Michelle

A MINSTREL® BOOK
Published by Pocket Books

Simon & Schuster Mail Order Dept. BWB
200 Old Tappan Rd., Old Tappan, N.J. 07675

Please send me the books I have checked above. I am enclosing $_____(please add $0.75 to cover the postage and handling for each order. Please add appropriate sales tax). Send check or money order–no cash or C.O.D.'s please. Allow up to six weeks for delivery. For purchase over $10.00 you may use VISA: card number, expiration date and customer signature must be included.

Name _____

Address _____

City _____ State/Zip _____

VISA Card # _____ Exp.Date _____

Signature _____

1033-28